Yearning In The Mountains

Greene Mountain Boys

Olivia T. Turner

Copyright© 2023 by Olivia T. Turner.
All rights reserved. No part of this book may be reproduced or transmitted in any form or by any means, electronic or mechanical, including emailing, photocopying, printing, recording, or by any information storage and retrieval system, without permission in writing from the author. For permission requests, email Olivia@oliviatturner.com

This is a work of fiction. Any resemblance to actual events, businesses, companies, locales or persons, living or dead, is entirely coincidental.
Contains explicit love scenes and adult language.
18+

www.OliviaTTurner.com

Edited by Karen Collins Editing
Cover Design by Olivia T. Turner

To my neighbor Cynthia.
Who loves watching the shirtless neighborhood landscaping
guys as much as I do.

Chapter One

Vivian

"Where are you now?" my mother asks through my headphones while we video chat. I just called her and my dad from the back of my Uber.

"I just arrived in the Greene Mountains," I tell them. "I'm heading to the rental cabin now."

"It doesn't look very sanitary," my mother says as she scrunches her nose up and looks all around me. My dad lowers the Wall Street Journal and looks at the screen for the first time. "They didn't have a limousine for you?"

"It's the mountains, Mom, not Paris."

"I still don't understand why you didn't go to Paris," she says, shaking her head. "It's Fashion Week."

"I've been to Paris a hundred times," I tell her as my dad goes back to his paper. "I've never been to the mountains."

In fact, I've never really been in nature. My parents are

all about cities. Milan, Tokyo, Montreal, Buenos Aires, Barcelona, Dubai—I've been to them all. My family vacations growing up were all about luxury, socialites, and concrete. I never saw a tree unless it was growing out of a sidewalk.

Once, I asked my parents if we could go camping instead of flying to London for a week. My mother scoffed and said that camping is for people with no taste.

"Or no money," my father added.

London was amazing, so were all of the other vacations (I'm not complaining), but there was something about the wild mountains that intrigued me. Sometimes, during stressful times at work, I find myself staring at the mountainous photos on my screensaver and wondering what if...

What if I gave up the fashion empire I started in Manhattan and moved out here for good?

But then the phone rings or Martin barges into my office with the crisis of the hour and the thought disappears as quickly as it came.

"We took you to Zurich that one time for the Holidays," my mother says, looking offended. "Remember, Jack? We rented that chalet with the broken hot tub and that slovenly property manager was such a jerk about it."

"I remember," my father mumbles as he reads.

That's not quite the way I remember it, but whatever. My mom was such a bitch to the guy and expected him to come fix it immediately even though it was Christmas Eve.

"It's not too late to turn back and fly somewhere reasonable," my mother says. "You're too pretty to be eaten by a bear. Don't you agree, Jack?"

"Much too pretty," Dad mumbles.

I sigh as I fight the urge to roll my eyes.

"You're breaking up," I lie. "I better go."

"The reception here is fine," she says. "Why don't you jet over to Cabo San Lucas if you need some mountains? You can rent a villa on the—"

I hit the little red X on my screen and my parents disappear.

I need a break from them as much as I need a break from work. We live in the same building on the same floor.

I don't remember ever giving my mother a key to my place, but she has one and she uses it daily. She's always popping over. Always commenting, criticizing, driving me crazy. I can't take it anymore.

I would never have chosen to live in the same city, let alone the same building as her, but when I told them I was moving out, they rented an apartment on the same floor as them without telling me. It was a big surprise.

Surprise! You're never getting away from us!

What was I supposed to do? Give up an amazing fully-paid apartment in Manhattan? I was starting a business and trying to save every cent I could. It would have been stupid and irresponsible to turn it down, so I didn't.

And I've been regretting it ever since.

"First time in Montana?" the Uber driver asks, breaking the silence. He's an older man with long scraggly hair and an old ripped T-shirt so dirty that I would be ashamed to wear it while painting.

"Huh? Yeah. First time in the mountains."

He glances at me through the rearview mirror. "When I pulled up, I thought you'd be staying at the Greene Mountain Lodge."

"Why is that?"

"On account of the pretty clothes and fancy suitcases. It's the most luxurious spot for miles."

"Oh," I say with a forced laugh. "I rented a nice place on Bearskin Mountain."

"There ain't no nice places on Bearskin Mountain, lady. Unless of course you're staying with Duncan Dove, but he never has visitors."

Now, I'm starting to get nervous.

I pull up the listing as he turns onto a dirt road. We're surrounded by tall trees and thick vegetation. My back presses into the seat of his pickup truck as we start to drive up a steep incline.

"Here," I say as I find the luxurious cabin and show it to him.

He stops the truck and looks at it for a long moment.

"That's the address," he says as he checks the GPS on his phone, "but I ain't never heard of a place like that up here."

My muscles twitch as I glance out the window.

Shit.

This is a new rental site that I've never used before and the listing didn't have any reviews.

No, it can't be...

It's probably just a new building and who is this guy anyway? There's no way he knows every piece of property in this vast mountain range.

"I'm sure it's going to be fine."

"If you say so," he says with a shrug as he hands my phone back.

I guess I can always head into town and stay at the Greene Mountain Lodge if the place turns out to be a scam.

He continues driving up the mountain and I cling to the handle on the door as I get bumped and rocked around.

The scenery is spectacular, but I can't really focus on that right now. I have a bad feeling in my gut about this. It takes another half an hour or so to wind around the mountain before the tip of a roof pokes out of the trees up ahead.

"You were right," the driver says with a chuckle. "There is a place up here."

I sink into the seat while exhaling in relief. Thank goodness for that.

But as he drives up to it, the panic returns. It doesn't look anything like the photos. It's deserted, rundown, and falling apart.

The luxurious cabin that I booked was constructed with full logs and has a large wraparound porch that looks out onto the stunning mountainous view.

This piece of shit cabin has a blue plastic tarp stapled over the rotting wood and the porch is littered with trash.

"It doesn't look much like the pictures," the driver says as he parks the truck.

"You think?!" I snap as I start to hyperventilate. "Is that a freaking hole in the roof?!"

Oh my god, it is! There's a huge hole in the goddamn roof!

I can't stay here.

"Well, let's get you settled in," the driver says as he steps out of the truck.

"Wait!" I nearly scream.

Either he doesn't hear me or he ignores me, but whatever the case, he walks to the back of his truck as I stare at the cabin in horror.

Oh no. This is my worst nightmare. The windows are filthy. Two of them are cracked. The chimney has disintegrated and its bricks have fallen onto the sunken in roof.

The grass is so tall around the place that it looks like the earth is in the process of reabsorbing it into the ground.

Trust me, nobody will miss this hellhole when it's gone besides the termites.

A knock on the window makes me jump.

"Come on out, Miss."

He opens the door and I cling to my seatbelt. "I can't stay here."

"Well, you can't stay *there*," he says, pointing into his truck. "I gotta head back to work."

"You are at work," I say in a desperate tone. "I'm *paying* you."

"This is just a side hustle," he says with his hands on his hips. "My real job is cutting down trees. The boss lets me do this on my lunch hour when business is light, but there's a tree that needs cutting on that mountain down there and I gotta get to it before dinner or my boss is going to whip my ass."

"Can you drop me off in town?"

He shakes his head and spits on the ground. "Not going that way."

"I'll make it worth your while," I say as I open my purse. Shit, I only have a ten on me. I shove it at him, hoping he'll take it.

He does.

I nearly cry, I'm so relieved. I don't have to stay in this murder cabin. I'll be in a luxurious cabin with a bathtub, room service, and a king-sized bed before I know it.

"You should take some pictures of this place and send it to that company," he says. "Might be you can get a refund for all that money you spent."

"Great idea!" I say as I hop out of the truck with my phone in my hand.

They'll have a hard time refusing a refund when I show them a picture of the freaking hole in the roof.

This place is even worse up close. There's a ton of water damage and there doesn't seem to be any electricity. Is that an outhouse?!

Oh my god, it is!

I walk over in disbelief, taking photos of it from every angle. It's *disgusting*.

I'm sooo happy I don't have to use that thing. I would die.

What was I thinking wanting to stay in the wilderness? I guess my mother was right—I'm not made for this part of the world.

Although, besides the horror cabin, the scenery is quite spectacular. It makes my—

"What?!"

I gasp as I whip my head around when I hear an engine start.

The driver is behind the wheel, giving me an apologetic look. "Sorry, lady. Gotta go!"

"No!" I screech as I run over. "You can't leave me here!"

"You'll be fine," he shouts back as his truck starts rolling. "There's a river down there with some fresh fish in it and you can drink the water too."

"What?!" I scream as he drives away, leaving my Louis Vuitton suitcases in his dust. "Come back! Please!!"

He doesn't stop.

My heart beats frantically as I watch his truck disappear down the steep road that we just drove up.

He just left. Like that. What a jerk!

I have to call another Uber.

Oh shit.

There's no reception on my phone. I try and try, but getting nothing but a frozen screen no matter what I do and no matter how high I hold it.

"What do I do?" I ask no one in particular as I look around in horror. "What the heck am I supposed to do now?"

A landline.

The word just pops into my head.

"Yes!" Maybe there's a landline phone in the cabin. I can call the lodge and offer them a gazillion dollars to send someone to pick me up. I'll leave this place, stay in a gorgeous suite, and leave all of this behind me. It will be nothing more than an amusing little anecdote I can tell at some fancy Manhattan parties.

I just have to... go in.

Gulp.

I take a deep breath, wrap my sweater around my head in case there are any bats hanging from the ceiling that are thinking about getting stuck in my hair, and slowly shuffle over to the porch.

With my phone's flashlight on, I carefully step over the rotting planks of wood and head to the front door. It's off the hinges and just leaning against the open doorway. Of course, it is.

I lift it and lean it against the cabin.

"Hello?" I say nervously as I look around the dark place, flashing my weak phone light around. "Anyone home?"

There are freaking *plants* growing *inside* this cabin. All the water leaking in from the ceiling mixed with the rotting leaves and it's created a whole ecosystem in here.

My hopes for finding a working landline diminish by the second.

I still haven't stepped foot in the place. Not sure I'm going to either.

When I flash my phone's light into the corner and see eyes reflecting back at me, I scream.

And run.

And curse.

A lot of cursing.

I curse the scammer who listed this place, the driver who left me hanging, and most of all, I curse myself.

What was I thinking? *Really?*

I thought that I would become one with nature and have a spiritual awakening. This is anything but!

I'm still breathing heavily with my heart pounding as I grab my suitcases and head for the road. I don't care if I have to walk all freaking night, I'm leaving this place. I'm not staying here for another second.

I drag my two big heavy suitcases down the dirt road and I never look back.

After an hour, I'm dying. My shoulders are killing me, my feet hurt, I'm hot, sweaty, hungry, cranky, and one of the wheels on my suitcase broke off, so I'm half dragging, half rolling it down this stupid mountain.

Just when I think that I might not make it, I see a dirt road turning off this cursed road and my body perks up.

"Is that...?"

There are fresh tire tracks in the dirt. Could it be?

With nothing to lose, I head down the road.

"Oh my god!" I whisper when I see the cabin coming into view a few minutes later. "Oh, fuck yes!"

It's the log cabin from the photos!

The nice luxurious one with the beautiful wraparound porch.

It wasn't a scam. It's all real!

I leave my suitcases on the dirt road and run the rest of the way, squealing in joy as my brown hair flows in the wind behind me.

I'm so happy that tears flow down my cheeks.

I run right up to the front door and pause when I see the address. It's different from the listing, but that's just a clerical mistake. This is *the* house! *My* house for the *week!*

The door is unlocked, so I head right in.

"Hello?" I call out as I kick off my shoes and look around.

It's beautiful in here. Absolutely perfect.

This place is getting five stars from me as soon as I can get my hands on an Internet connection.

The owners left a sweater on the chair beside the kitchen table and some food out, but it's not a big deal. They didn't clean the coffee pot either—it's half full—but I'm not about to complain about little things like that after the last place.

I just head straight for the huge bathroom with the giant walk-in shower, stripping my sweaty clothes off along the way.

I'm butt naked by the time I step on the warm tiles.

"Yes," I whisper as I open the glass door of the shower. "Fuck, yes!"

I turn on the warm water, step under the huge rain showerhead, and moan as I start the best shower of my life.

Chapter Two

Duncan

"What the hell is that?" I mutter to myself as I pull onto my private road and see the strange sight before me. "That's a new one."

I park my truck and stare at the two pieces of overturned luggage in my way, wondering how the hell they got there.

My first thought is that they fell out of an airplane, but they wouldn't be in this good of condition if that happened. They'd be slammed into pancakes and all that's wrong with them is a little dirt and one missing wheel.

I step out of my truck and head over, wondering if someone is playing a prank on me or something.

Louis Vuitton.

I don't know too much about designer brands, but even I can tell that these suitcases cost a pretty penny.

I straighten one up, pull down the zipper, and peek in at

the clothes inside. They're women's clothes. Same with the other bag. Interesting.

But what the hell are they doing here?

I toss them into the back of my pickup truck, look around, and then continue to my house.

No car in the driveway, nothing else out of the ordinary, weird.

But then I walk into the house and hear the shower running...

...and see a pair of women's shoes that weren't there when I left this morning. They're not set nicely beside each other like mine are—one is beside the closet and the other is in the hallway, like she kicked them off and didn't care where they landed.

I take one and inspect it a little closer. It looks so tiny in my big hand, like some princess wandered into an ogre's lair in a fairytale and forgot her shoe.

I drop it and move forward with an annoyed grimace on my face.

You move to a quiet part of the country, to a mountain with only one other property on it that's abandoned, and people still bother you.

Why can't everyone just leave me the hell alone?

My heart pounds in my chest as I walk down the hall, stepping over the trail of clothing. Socks, pants, a shirt, and... ladies' underwear.

I bend over, pick up the pair of pink panties with two fingers, look at them, and then drop them back down.

Whoever is in my bathroom is as naked as the day they were born.

I want to know why the hell they picked my place to barge into, but more than anything, I just want them gone.

She starts singing.

"Oh my god," I whisper as I shake my head and move forward.

I peek into the bathroom and see her in the shower. A pink silhouette hidden by mist and foggy glass. Steam rises above the showerhead and spills over. I swallow hard as I watch the blur of her moving body while listening to her beautiful voice.

I want her out of here.

That's what I keep telling myself, but my body is frozen as I listen to her captivating melodic singing. I stay until she turns the water off and the daze she has me under breaks.

"What the hell are you doing?" I angrily whisper to myself. "She needs to go."

I hurry back into the kitchen, stepping over her clothes along the way, and sit down on one of the stools at my giant granite island and wait for her.

She hums as she steps out of *my* shower like she owns the freaking place.

See, this is why I don't like people. They're nothing but trouble. They use you, take what they want, and then dump you to the curb as soon as the day comes when you can no longer give them what they want.

It's better to be alone. It's easier. It's the only way to live.

And as soon as this insolent, disrespectful, arrogant girl is done with my shower, I'm going to kick her out and be in blissful solitude once again.

I cross my arms and glare forward and she walks down the hall, singing some annoying song I've never heard before.

My chest tightens and my breath gets lodged somewhere in my throat when I see her step into the kitchen wearing nothing but a towel wrapped around her head like a turban.

She's naked.

And I can't... fucking... breathe...

Time slows. Each second stretches to an eternity.

The laws of physics warp around this woman. She's a universe onto herself.

Her intense striking beauty and raw sexuality grip me in a way I've never been gripped before. It squeezes my heart and won't let go. I'm stunned as I stare at this lovely princess in awe.

I really do feel like an ogre next to her.

My eyes take in as much as they can before she'll inevitably see me and cover up.

Her face is pure beauty, but that body... pure heaven.

My eyes slide down her slender neck onto her bare chest. Her round naked tits are hanging down with those perky little pink nipples in full mouthwatering view. Waterdrops cling to her flawless skin as I feel my obsession with her taking root deep in my core.

For the first time in my life, I *need* a woman. I need her like a drowning man needs air.

My eyes continue down her beautiful stomach and onto her round hips that I can't wait to grab onto and test out their sturdiness. Those hips were made for childbearing and they were made for *me*.

I fight back a growl as I slide my eyes onto the tuft of brown hair between her legs. Possession fills every inch of my body as I get a glimpse of her pussy with those soft-looking pink lips. I want to throw her onto this island and spread her legs with my rough hands to see every inch of it, but I can't.

Because she starts screaming.

Full-on panicked scream.

"What the fuck?!" she hollers so loud it feels like my eardrums are being pierced.

She lunges forward, grabs my dirty breakfast plate off the counter, and covers her tits with it. But then she realizes I can still see her little kitty, so she moves the plate down to cover that instead. When I look at her big beautiful tits, she yanks the plate back up, and then down, and then she just launches it at me with a scream.

It sails over my shoulder and shatters into a hundred pieces on the floor behind me.

With all this going on, I never take my eyes off her. I can't. It's physically impossible for me to look away.

She grabs her clothes off the floor and holds them against her, hiding all of her sexy little pink parts. But I can still see those delicious hips peeking out, those slick shoulders with her mesmerizing collarbone, and the wild look in her stunning blue eyes.

"Get out of here!" she screams at me like a wild animal.

"Get out of my own house?" I ask calmly.

"Yes!" she screeches back. "You're not supposed to be here! I rented it fair and square!"

I'm so confused right now.

"What?"

"I'm getting changed in the bathroom," she shouts. "*Don't* follow me!"

She turns and I get a quick glimpse of that beautiful ass before she covers it with her shirt. The sexy inviting image of those cheeks burn into my brain as she disappears down the hall, those little princess feet pitter-pattering on my floor.

The bathroom door slams shut and I'm left sitting here

with my head spinning, wondering how my life could be so turned upside down in an instant.

I drop my eyes and realize my cock is rock hard. It's aching for this woman. It was *made* for this woman.

My heart pounds like never before as I wait for her to return.

The dark side of me—the animalistic side—is screaming at me to go in there and take what's mine. I squeeze my eyes shut and try to focus on my breathing. I have to calm my nerves down.

My hands are fucking shaking and they never shake.

This feeling of need is so overwhelming. It's so unexpected.

I'm thirty-eight years old and never had an experience like this. I've never needed anyone, never had anyone, never wanted anyone.

But now, everything is different. I want *her*.

It's not just her naked body that's doing it to me. No, it runs deeper than that.

She's my twin flame.

I know it because the burn is so damn sweet.

We share the same soul, me and her. It's the only thing that can explain this intense magnetic attraction and instant connection.

I knew it as soon as I looked into those soft blue eyes. I knew we were meant to be together. All the rest... those luscious curves... that sweet sensual body... that's all just a bonus. I know I would be feeling the same if she was bundled up in a subzero parka.

"This is *so* unprofessional," she shouts as she comes storming back down the hallway in tight black pants and a long loose shirt. I swallow hard as I slowly look her up from her bare toes to her wavy wet hair. She's breathtaking.

"I'm going to give you a zero star rating," she says with her body all tight and rigid she's so mad, "a review so bad it will make you a pariah on that site and every other site you list on. I'm going to complain to the company, the rental board if there is one, and the police! Yeah, that's right! I'm going to have you arrested for being a pervert!"

I can't help but grin as I watch the fire sizzling inside her. She's incredible.

"I'm the pervert?" I ask, not being able to help myself. "*You* were the one who flashed *me*."

"*I* flashed *you*?!" she screeches with her hands balled up into fists. "Oh, you must think you're really fucking funny, don't you?!"

"I don't know what to think right now," I say, staring at her in both awe and confusion. I'm still not sure what the hell she's talking about.

She stares at me for a beat and then grabs the closest thing to her—a washcloth off the stove—and throws it at me. "*Get the fuck out of here!*"

I stand up and back away with my hands up, trying to let her know that I'm not a threat. She's glaring at me with her fists on her hips and a stern look on her face. Her jaw is clenched tight and she's shaking with anger.

"I think you're in the wrong house," I tell her in a soft voice. "I've lived here for six years and I've never rented it out before."

That tight jaw loosens a little and she suddenly doesn't look so sure of herself.

"You haven't?"

I shake my head. "No."

"Stay right there," she demands, pointing at me as she walks around the room to get to her purse beside the door.

She grabs it and yanks her phone out.

"Isn't this your place?" she says as she thrusts the screen at me.

I slowly walk over and look at it.

"That's my house, but it's the wrong address."

"Are you Kyle Kline?"

"Duncan Dove," I tell her. "I've never heard of a Kyle Kline before in my life."

Her face drops as she looks at the phone like she can't quite comprehend what's happening.

"I paid good money to rent this place," she says. "Is there another house on the mountain or something? Maybe the same builder built two?"

"I was the builder and I only built this one."

"But the address..."

"Is for the abandoned house up the road. I think a family of raccoons lives in it now. Although, they might have moved out over the winter."

"No, they're still there," she says with her shoulders slumping down. "I saw them."

She looks so defeated as she shoves her phone into her purse.

"I got scammed."

"Looks like it," I say as my eyes roam down to those lips. They look so soft and luscious. I want to feel them. I want to taste them. I want them to be all mine.

"Are you still going to have me arrested?" I ask her.

She looks apologetic as she looks up at me with those big blue Bambi eyes. "Are you going to have me arrested for breaking and entering?"

"Don't forget the indecent exposure."

She drops her head into her hands and groans. "Oh my god, this is so embarrassing."

Embarrassing? This is the most fun I've had in years.

"I'm sorry," she says as she suddenly rushes to the door. "You'll never see me again."

"Whoa!" I say, panicked at the thought. "Where are you going? I didn't see a car in the driveway."

"I'll walk to town."

"It's going to take you all night," I say, desperate for her to stay. "And once the darkness comes, the hungry bears do too."

"Bears?" she asks with a gulp.

The threat of bears always gets the city folk all riled up. They think a ravenous bear is hiding around every tree up here just waiting to try and catch a tourist wandering by.

"Yeah," I say, laying it on thick. "It's going to be dark soon and you don't want to be out there in the dark."

She gulps. "Can I... use your phone? To call an Uber or something?"

"This isn't New York City," I tell her. "You can't expect someone out here to pop up anytime you need it."

Her eyes drop to the floor. "Do you know how I can get to the Greene Mountain Lodge?"

"I'll take you."

"You will? After what I did?"

The only thing she did was give me the view of a lifetime and steal my heart.

"Well, I can't exactly let you walk now, can I?"

"Thank you so much. If you had a listing, I'd give you five stars!"

"Give me a second," I tell her as I head into my bedroom. "Grab something from the fridge if you're hungry."

Her sensual smell is still lingering in the hallway making me all lightheaded and woozy.

I can't let this girl go.

No fucking way.

I quietly close the door and dial the number.

"*Greene Mountain Lodge, Tina speaking,*" the voice on the other end says. "*What do you want?*"

"Do you have any rooms available for tonight?"

"*We have nine rooms,*" she says in a tone that makes her sound like she's bored beyond belief. "*Do you want one?*"

"I want all nine," I tell her with my pulse racing. "Put them all on my card."

Chapter Three

Vivian

"How did you know I'm from New York City?" I ask as we're driving down the mountain.

Duncan looks at me with confusion in his brown eyes. "What do you mean?"

"At the house when I asked about an Uber, you said 'This isn't New York City.'" I give my best deep gruff sounding voice as I imitate him.

He grins in amusement. It makes my heart flitter.

This guy is *seriously* hot.

I love his beard. It's so thick and manly with the perfect shade of brown. The hair on his head is a little darker with a few thin streaks of gray mixed in. He's older than me, I can tell, but that doesn't matter to me at all. I guess I have a thing for older men now.

I barely come up to his chin and he's built as solid as this mountain. Every inch of him is thick muscle. My eyes keep involuntary darting to his big broad shoulders and massive chest. I wonder how strong he is. He looks like he could easily pick me up.

He's wearing a light gray Polo shirt with the sleeves squeezed tight around his firm round biceps and a pair of jeans that hug his thick muscular thighs and nice ass perfectly.

But it's his tattoos that are really getting me flustered. They run along his powerful arms as if his arms aren't already beautiful enough, and up his thick neck. I can't stop looking at them and admiring every intricate detail of the gorgeous ink.

Even in New York City with all of the models and celebrities, this man would turn every head while walking down the crowded sidewalk

If I had to show my naked body to a stranger again, I could think of worse people to show it to than him.

I still can't believe I did that. He must think I'm a total idiot.

I don't even want to think about it.

He glances over at me and my heart starts pounding. He's got this way of looking at me with his dark brown eyes that makes me go all weak and wobbly. That's a feeling I'm not used to.

In my world, *I'm* the boss. I'm the one who makes people get all trembly inside when I pull them into my office for a stern word. I'm always the calm one. I'm never the one who's all shaky.

"I didn't know you lived in New York," he says as he turns the wheel, maneuvering the truck around a bend. My eyes drop to his thick tattooed forearms and then slide down to his big powerful hand that's gripping the steering wheel. "It was just a coincidence. That's where you live?"

"Yup!" I say proudly. I'm expecting him to be impressed—people normally are when you tell them you live in New York—but he just frowns as he turns to me.

"Why would you want to live there?"

"Because it's only the most amazing city in the world," I say indignantly.

"I don't doubt that," he says as he turns back to the road. "But it's still just a city. Doesn't beat living out here."

I'm about to bite back, but the view opens up to a stunning bit of scenery and my words get lost as I stare at it in awe. We're up high and the view of the mountains seems to go on forever into the distance. There's so much blue sky without any skyscrapers or cranes or airplanes disrupting the spectacular view. Thousands of trees paint the landscape in all sorts of shades of green. A river cuts through it all, slowly flowing over the round peaceful rocks that have been there since before New York even existed.

"You don't get views like this in New York," he says as he slows his truck to a stop. The window is open and the air is so crisp. It's so clean and fresh. You don't get air like this either.

"Maybe," I say, not wanting to give in to this sexy stranger just yet. "But have you seen the city from the top of the Empire State Building? Or, from the Statue of Liberty?"

"I can't say that I have."

"So," I say with a humph. "You don't really know what you're talking about then."

"Maybe," he says. "But I do know that you don't get the same peaceful feeling in your soul when you're looking at concrete, cars, and millions of anxious people running around as you do looking at that."

I turn back to the striking view and a little bit of the bottled-up stress and anxiety I've been feeling seeps out of me. This place does seem to have a calming effect on my body.

I wonder what it would be like to live here.

"I'm thinking of moving," I say. It just blurts out of me. I haven't told anyone that, even my parents.

"Oh yeah?"

I sigh as I stare at a bird swooping through the vast sky, looking freer than I've ever felt in my life.

"I spent the last eight years of my life building a fashion brand," I tell him, exhausted just thinking about it. "And I got an offer from a big company to buy it."

"That's impressive."

"You haven't even heard the number they offered."

Five million dollars. I couldn't believe it when I saw the number.

I can cash in with that incredible amount or I can spend the next ten years growing it into a nine-figure brand. The stress might kill me though and I would never have time to start a family, which is also one of my life goals. I really don't know what to do.

"That's why I'm out here," I say as he starts driving again, rolling down the mountain. "I wanted some peace and tranquility for a week to think it over."

"You came to the right place. You can't get more tranquil than the Greene Mountains."

"What do you think I should do?"

"Me?" he asks, looking at me with amusement. "We just met. You want my opinion?"

"As an impartial observer, sure."

He tilts his head. "I wouldn't say I'm impartial."

What does *that* mean?

"But I'll give you my opinion. I think you should sell."

Yearning In The Mountains

I turn in my seat and study his face as he drives. "How come?"

"Because you want to sell."

I laugh. "And how do you know that?"

"Because you're here, thinking it over. If you still had the passion and fire for your company, you wouldn't have thought twice about turning it down. A part of you is searching for more out of life."

I open my mouth to retort, but there are no words. I just exhale long and hard as I turn back to the mountains, thinking about what he said.

Maybe this hot rugged mountain man has a point.

"This is the Greene Mountain Lodge?" I say, staring at it in shock as Duncan drives toward it. It's stunning, luxurious, and exactly what I had in mind. "This is where I should have stayed. I didn't even know about it."

"It's the hottest place in town," he says as he pulls into the parking lot and parks his big truck. "It's usually all booked up."

"I can see why," I say as I take in the sweeping view of the luxurious stone and log building situated at the base of a majestic mountain close to a sparkling lake.

I'm really hoping there's an available room as we walk into the spectacular lobby with the giant stone fireplace. The doorman welcomes us and I suddenly realize that we must look like a couple walking in to get a room together.

I get all tingly from the notion. I wonder what that would be like…

…walking into a room with Duncan. Those big arms picking me up and carrying me through the door, tossing me onto the bed, the view of him pulling that shirt off in one swift motion as he walks over revealing all of that tattooed skin pulled tight over his clenched rippling muscles. The insane heat flowing through my body as my eyes slide down his hard chiseled abs and settle on the long thick shape of his erection jutting out against his...

"Are you okay?" Duncan asks, stopping as he looks at me.

"What? Yeah! Why? Huh?"

He puts his hand on my shoulder as he looks at me with concern. The feel of his hand on me sends a shiver rippling down my spine. I hope he didn't feel that, but I know that he did.

"Yeah," I say as he patiently waits for me to regain my composure. "It's just... a really nice lodge."

I swallow hard, shake the dirty thoughts out of my head, and quickly head over to the reception desk. Duncan hangs back, letting me handle this on my own.

A pair of identical twins are working at the computers. Their name tags say Tina and Tiffany and they both have the same strange black bob haircut and thick black-rimmed glasses. Neither of them looks up at me as I walk over.

"Hello," I say to Tina after a long moment of standing there awkwardly.

I can feel the contempt dripping off her as she slowly looks up at me.

Geez... And people think New Yorkers are rude. No one working in customer service is this bad in the Big Apple.

"I was wondering if I could book a room," I say in the friendliest voice I can muster.

"For when?"

"For right now?" I say with a forced smile.

"Can't. We're all booked."

Oh shit.

"But... Do you have anything? Anything at all?"

"We had nine rooms available."

"Okay," I say, perking up as I get my hopes up.

"But someone just booked them all."

"Shit," I say, deflating once again. "That's unlucky."

"Super unlucky," Tina says bluntly. "I guess you're going to have to sleep in the bus station or something."

"Or, in the park," her co-worker *slash* twin sister says.

"Just watch out for the Sheriff," Tina adds. "He's quick with the taser."

I don't want to sleep anywhere but in a comfy king-sized bed.

"Is there another place in town?" I ask, desperate for a room.

"The inn," Tina says as she turns back to her computer. "But it's always full. It only has six rooms."

Oh, crappers. They're probably all booked.

"Would you mind calling the inn and asking if they have a room available?" I ask desperately.

The twins look at each other as if saying, 'Get a load of this girl.'

"Please!" I say, threading my fingers together as I plead with them.

Tina rolls her eyes dramatically as she picks up her phone. She puts in the number and then sighs with contempt as she waits for the other end to pick up.

"*Hello*," I hear the lady on the other end say.

"Do you have any rooms available?" Tina rudely asks.

The woman says something that I can't quite hear. Tina hangs up on her mid-sentence.

"They're booked."

"Oh, what am I going to do?" I mutter as I look around in a panic. "Are there any Airbnb's in the area or rentals that I could take? Anything?"

Tina frowns as she looks at me.

"Please," I beg. "I got scammed by a fake rental and I don't know what to do."

"Let me ask for some help," Tina says after a long while.

"Thank you!"

She turns to her sister. "Hey, Tiffany."

"Yes, Tina."

"Are we travel agents?"

Tiffany shakes her head. "No, we're not."

"And do we book rentals around town?"

"No, we book rooms in this lodge only."

"Final question," Tina says in a sarcastic tone. "What if a random person walks in off the street who is *not* a client of this lodge and wants us to fix all of her horrible life planning?"

I sigh as I watch their little routine, feeling like I'm going to be sick.

"*Hmmm*," Tiffany says, thinking about it. "I guess in that case, you can either help the person or you can tell them to piss off. Choice is yours."

"Thanks, Tiffany."

"No problem, Tina."

Tina turns back to me and looks at me for a long moment. "Piss off."

I sigh as I turn and leave, feeling more defeated than ever.

I guess I'll go and sleep with the raccoons in that abandoned cabin after all. Maybe I'll get lucky and it won't rain all week.

"Any rooms?" Duncan asks as I shuffle over with my head hanging down.

"None."

"That sucks."

"Thanks for your help," I say, trying to force out a smile, but it's damn near impossible right now. "I don't want to take up any more of your time, so I'll get my bags and you're free to go."

"Stay with me."

My eyes dart up to his. "What?"

"I have an extra room in my house," he says as those dark brown eyes bore into me like they're gripping my soul. "Stay with me."

"But..."

"You're not sleeping in the park or the bus station all week. You're staying with me."

He says it with such confidence like the decision is already made. My body leans toward him. I so badly want to say yes.

"But you're a stranger."

He shrugs those big sexy shoulders. "What are you afraid of?"

"You being a creep."

He smiles and my knees nearly buckle. "I already saw you naked."

"Don't remind me," I say as my cheeks heat up. "I'm trying to forget about that little incident."

"I'll give you your privacy."

I nibble my bottom lip as I stare at him, unsure of what to do.

"I can just close my eyes and see it all over again," he says with a grin. My cheeks heat up even more.

"Okay, don't do that," I quickly say. "But it's not just your eyes I'm worried about. What about your hands?"

He holds them out, palms up. "Touch them. They're not so bad."

I suck in a sharp breath as I slowly reach out and feel them. My fingertips examine his skin, tracing the long deep lines. His hands are softer than I thought they would be. His fingers are so thick and long. His palm so big. They feel so strong, like he could crush rocks with ease.

The tingling in my stomach moves down and settles between my legs as I explore his masculine hands. The flush in my cheeks moves along my neck and onto my upper chest as I wonder what these hands would feel like on my body.

"See?" he says when I finally release them. "Harmless."

My body is aching as I stand here, more turned on than I've ever been in my life. I'm twenty-four, but I'm still a virgin. No one has ever managed to get me all worked up like this. Never in my whole life.

Who the hell is this guy and why is my body reacting to him in such a strong way? I don't get it.

"You're staying with me."

That firm voice. The possessive way he looks at me. It's all so overwhelming. It's all so enticing.

"Stay with me, Vivian. You won't regret it."

I swallow hard as my head nods all on its own.

"Okay," I say in a breathless tone. "I'll stay with you."

I'm a virgin now, but who knows if I'll still be one by the end of the week.

All bets are off.

I'm in unchartered territory now...

Chapter Four

Vivian

"Mr. Duncan Donuts!" the elderly cashier at the grocery store says with a big smile when he sees Duncan and me arrive with a cart of food. He's a small wiry guy who kind of reminds me of my weird uncle who I haven't seen in years. "And you must be the donut hole! Wait, that didn't sound right. I swear it didn't sound perverted in my head."

"Don't worry about it," I say with a laugh as I take some of the fresh veggies out of the cart and put them on the conveyor belt. "And by the way, I'm more of a fancy latte."

He lets out a sharp high-pitched laugh that makes me jump back in shock.

I look up at Duncan and he smiles knowingly.

"Hey Warren, this is Vivian," Duncan tells him. "She's from New York City."

Warren whistles low. "And what are you doing in our little town, Vivian?"

"Escaping," I say with a chuckle.

"Well, you couldn't have picked a better place to escape to," Warren says as he scans our groceries. "We're about as far from New York City as we are to the moon."

"I'm starting to see that," I say as I watch Duncan putting groceries into his reusable bags. No one knows your name in New York. I've been to the same grocery store for ages and none of the cashiers even recognize me, let alone know my name. It must be nice to see familiar faces once in a while.

He rings us up and I pull out my wallet to pay, but Duncan stops me. "Not going to happen," he grunts in a tone that's final. I don't even try to fight him. I know that's going to be a battle I'll definitely lose.

"Enjoy your escape, Vivian," Warren says as we get ready to leave. "And come visit our little town again. We don't have enough fancy lattes around here. Only regular ole coffees."

That's what I like about it. The people are so down-to-earth and real. Everyone is so superficial where I'm from. They all have a personal brand they're desperately trying to cultivate, and they *all* want something from me.

"Here you go," Duncan says to Warren as he hands over a heaping bag of food. "For Wendy."

"I'll add it to the pile," Warren says as he takes it and puts it under the register. "Have a good day now."

I can't help but watch Duncan as we walk to his truck. It's around dinner time and the sun is starting its long summer descent. He looks good in the muted colors of the twilight. He looks good all the time.

The heavy grocery bags are hanging from his big hands,

his arms all flexed and hard. I swallow the excess saliva building in my mouth when I see a long vein running up his tattooed skin.

"Who's Wendy?" I ask when we get to the truck.

He smiles sadly at me. "Just someone in town. Her husband died of a heart attack last week. She doesn't have a lot of money."

"Do you know her?"

"No."

"But you still helped her?"

He puts the bags of groceries into the flatbed of his truck and shrugs. "We help each other out around here."

I watch him, lost in thought as he walks over to my door and opens it.

"You don't have that kind of community in New York?"

He's teasing me.

"Not quite," I say, watching him as I walk over. His eyes never leave me as I step into his truck. "People are a little more self-centered where I'm from."

"That's a shame." He closes the door and walks around the front of the truck. My eyes are locked on him. He's so freaking hot. That body, that face, those eyes… I gotta get a picture of this man before I leave.

Maybe a few pictures. Oh! Maybe I can turn them into a calendar and put it on my office wall so I can gaze at him all day when I'm desperate for an escape from my life.

"So, you're here for a week," he says as he gets into the truck. "What do you like to do? Hiking? Kayaking? Riding horses?"

"I don't know," I say as I stare at my fidgeting hands. "I've never done any of it before."

"What do you mean? Have you ever left the city?"

"I've left New York," I say, flashing him a nervous smile.

"But I've never really been in a place like this before. I've always wanted to though. My parents never really liked nature."

"Alright," he says as he puts the truck into drive. "Then we're going to have a busy week."

"Why? What are we going to do?"

"All of it."

I'm really starting to crush hard on this hot mountain man. Not only is he gorgeous as hell, but he's a perfect gentleman too.

He cooked me a delicious dinner of honey garlic glazed salmon that he caught himself with a heaping side of fresh roasted vegetables. I never eat like this back home. It's always pre-packaged something or other microwaved to mediocrity. Served in front of the TV with a paper towel napkin.

We're sitting at the candlelit table finishing a bottle of wine.

I'm gazing into his sparkling brown eyes, getting a little too tipsy for my own good.

"Do you have family living nearby?" I ask, wanting to know everything about him. I want to know every detail about this intriguing man. My curiosity is off the charts.

He leans back and drops his eyes. "No," he says in a soft voice.

I'm waiting for him to expand, but he doesn't. "So, you're all alone up here?"

"Yeah." I think I hit a nerve or something. The easy smiles he's been giving me all night vanish. I hope I didn't upset him. I wonder what the story behind that is...

"I'll do the dishes," I say, trying to cut the awkward silence. "Since you cooked."

"I already did the dishes," he says, giving me one of those beautiful smiles again. It makes my chest all light and airy to see him like this. "There's nothing left to do."

"Then I should… get to… bed."

I don't really want to. I want to spend the whole night talking with this incredible stranger. Or, doing other things…

But it's our first night and I need some alone time to clear my head. I'm not thinking straight right now thanks to the bottle of wine and Duncan's devilish smile. I need some sleep and some distance to get my head screwed on right and to get this crush under control.

I thank him for dinner and then hurry off to my room, wondering if I'll be sleeping in the master bedroom by the end of the week.

Chapter Five

Duncan

"I think my kayak is broken!" Vivian screeches as it wobbles down the river.

I race forward, slicing my paddle into the water to get to my girl as quickly as I can.

She has a panicked look on her face as I slide up beside her, my kayak only a few inches from hers. "Is it supposed to be so wobbly? It keeps trying to tip me over!"

She's so adorable. I'm falling hard for her. With every second I'm in her presence, I fall a little bit deeper in love.

"You have to stabilize it with your hips."

Just the thought of her hips and the way she moves them makes me want to moan. This girl has been *killing* me since she arrived. I keep thinking of her body, standing there in my hallway completely naked... I'm desperate to see her like that again.

"Oh shit!" she shouts as a few little waves come by and rock her. I smile as I grab her kayak, stabilizing her.

"You're doing great," I tell her. "For a city girl."

"I'm going to be so wet by the end of the day."

That's the plan...

"Alright," she says as she straightens her back with a look of resolve in her gorgeous blue eyes. "I'll try again."

I sit in my kayak and watch as she begins to paddle. Her brown hair is tied back in a ponytail, which I love on her. It's the first time I've seen her hair pulled back with the enticing sight of her exposed neck and flawless face.

She's wearing aviator sunglasses, a big orange life jacket, a bikini under her shorts and tank top, and flip-flops. I want to go all ravenous caveman on her and rip it all off her body.

After a few minutes, she gets the hang of it and circles back to me with a triumphant smile on her stunning face.

"Not bad, huh?"

"You're amazing," I tell her.

"Stop teasing," she says, splashing me lightly with her paddle. "It's not so bad for a *city girl*."

We head down the river and she marvels at every spectacular sight we see. This is the most stunning river in Montana. The tall majestic mountains towering into the blue sky, the old trees watching from overhead, the sun sparkling off the water, the adorable animals scurrying along the shore, the families of ducks gliding on the water beside us, the sandy beaches around every bend—this river has it all.

She's watching everything in wonder, but I'm only watching her.

I know why she's here. Everything is so fast-paced in her world. Minutes, hours, days, weeks, months, years—they fly by in the city. Everyone is trying to optimize every second. They try to be productive every minute. And then what happens? Years fly by and your stressed-out psyche wonders what it was all for.

My girl is a success in that world, but I can tell she's yearning for something more. It's not enough for her. It's not making her happy.

She's a mountain girl who was born in the wrong spot.

Maybe she's not the best on a kayak yet, but I keep seeing the look in her eyes whenever I show her something new. I'm seeing her connect with nature for the very first time and it's endearing. It warms my heart.

It's my job this week to show her everything that nature has to offer. I have to present her with the beauty and tranquility of the mountains and hope that's enough for her to want to stay.

"Can you pass me my sandwich?" she asks as she paddles over.

"You want to eat now?" I ask as I open the cooler and pull out the sandwich I made this morning. "There's a great spot not too far up the river where we can set up a picnic."

She takes it from me and rips off a chunk of bread. "I just want to make friends with the ducks," she says as she hands the rest of the sandwich back to me.

I smile as I put it back in the cooler and watch her go.

It's a perfect day with the sun shining and the crystal-clear water warm enough to swim in. It feels like a little slice of heaven just for us.

The ducks are weary of her, but as soon as they spot that bread in her hand, they get a little bolder.

"I won't hurt you," she says in a soft voice as they glide toward her, still looking a little unsure.

I head over to join her as she breaks off some chunks

and starts tossing them in the water. The ducks eagerly scoop them up, racing to each spot where the bread lands.

I've never seen her look so happy. It makes my heart ache as I watch the pure joy on her face.

She tosses the last piece and then turns to me. "I want to give them my whole sandwich, but I'll be starving later."

"You can give them some of mine."

"Really?" she says, lighting up. "Hear that duckies? Duncan is going to share his lunch with you too!"

"Not all of it," I say with a grin as I hand her a chunk of bread.

It's worth going hungry to see her like this. If she's looking to connect with nature, then this is the place.

"That little one in the back isn't getting any," she says with a frown. "These bullies aren't letting her have a bite."

She launches the last piece as far as she can, trying to get it to the duck in the back. The motion of her arm makes her whole kayak wobble violently.

I grab it as she screams in surprise.

"I got you," I whisper as I pull her kayak next to mine. We're nice and close now.

She's breathing heavily as she looks at me. Even under those big sunglasses, I can tell she's looking at my mouth. I look at hers. Those lips are irresistible.

Our bodies come together on their own. Our lips like magnets as we both lean in.

My whole body ignites as our lips touch in a soft gentle kiss. Even though I'm desperate for her, I force myself to go slowly and gently.

Her lips part with a moan and I slide my tongue into her mouth, tasting her sweetness. She's fucking delicious.

I reach up and cup her jaw, pulling her forward as I explore her mouth with more urgency. The control I've been struggling to maintain begins to slip away with every sexy sound she makes. She holds onto my bicep as I deepen the kiss.

Her tongue slides against mine as our kayaks rock against each other. I can't believe I'm kissing this princess. I can't believe I'm this fucking lucky.

I slide my hand up the back of her neck and grab her ponytail. She moans sharply as I pull her head back to get her mouth right where I want it.

My dick is rock fucking hard by the time we pull away. I don't think I've ever been this hard in all my life.

We're both taking quick sharp breaths as my face hovers over hers. I can see the ravenous look on my face in the reflection of her sunglasses and it shocks me. I look like a man possessed for this woman.

"I wasn't sure about kayaking," she says with flushed cheeks and a shy smile, "but this is really fun."

She leans in to kiss me again, but she's not used to her kayak yet and she moves too abruptly. It rocks too much. She screams and grabs onto my arm, making it even worse as she yanks me down with her.

I thrust my hips to the side, desperately trying to hold us up, but the momentum is not on my side and we both tip over.

We slam into the warm water and go under.

Vivian. Save Vivian!

Those words roar through my head as I slip out of my kayak and reach for her.

But the water is only up to my navel, so she's not in any real danger. We both stand up as the warm water pours off us. She's staring at me in shock, not quite knowing what happened. It dawns on her when she sees our flipped kayaks and she starts laughing.

A little giggle at first, but then she's clinging onto me as she laughs harder—that beautiful sound making me fall even deeper in love with her, which I didn't think was possible.

"I guess that's what happens when you bring a city girl kayaking," she says as she leans into my soaked body and looks up at me with her bright blue eyes and wide smile.

I can't help but kiss her.

She hasn't realized that her sunglasses are in the river, but I don't want to waste this moment by looking for them. I'll buy her a new pair. I'll buy her a hundred pairs.

We come together—fitting so perfectly—and I take her mouth once again.

I'm laying my claim on this sexy little tongue and these soft luscious lips. They're mine now.

I'm never letting them go.

<hr />

Our lunch got ruined in the river, so I took Vivian to McArthur's for lunch. It's a nice little restaurant in town with an old jukebox and the best french fries in the area.

I was a bit worried it wouldn't be enough for her since she's from New York with all of the world-class restaurants and famous chefs, but she's loving it.

It brings a smile to my face as she looks around the place, marveling at all of the old shit hanging on the walls.

"Imagine having to plow a field by hand with that thing?" she says as she looks up at the old scythe hanging on the wall. "Mountain men must have been so tough back then." Her blue eyes dart to my big arms and she swallows hard. "I guess they still are."

April, the gruff waitress who's so rude she's practically a

Greene Mountain institution at this point, brings our drinks.

She eyes Vivian as she places her cherry Coke in front of her. "Where did you come from?" she asks in a flat tone.

"New York," Vivian answers with a gulp.

"I'm surprised a city girl is the one who got this hermit out of his shell."

"I'm not that much of a hermit," I say in a defensive tone.

She puts her hand on her hip and gives me a 'bitch please' look. "Then why are you always in here alone?"

"Because I've been waiting for you to ask me out."

She rolls her eyes. "The answer is no. Always no."

Vivian and I laugh as she shuffles away.

She takes a sip of her cherry Coke and makes a sexy little moan at the taste.

"Why are you out here all on your own?" she asks, studying me with those gorgeous analytical eyes. "I'm sorry, it's just... Aren't you lonely? How can you be so isolated?"

"How can *you* be so isolated and lonely?"

She jerks her head back, looking at me funny. "I'm surrounded by people all day. It's impossible for me to be lonely."

"Just because you're surrounded by people, doesn't mean you're not lonely. Are you seriously going to tell me you're not? I can tell that you've been feeling like you're missing something in your life."

She looks down at the table as she traces a circle on the thick wood with her fingertip. "Maybe a little..."

My girl doesn't have to finish the thought. I know. She felt like she was missing something until she met me.

I feel the same way.

That's what happens when soul mates find each other. Everything clicks into place.

"You asked me about my family last night."

She looks up at me through those long eyelashes. "Oh, you don't have to..."

"I want to." I want to be open and honest with her. I don't want there to be any secrets between us. We're soul mates and there's no place for that. I've never told anyone this, but I'll tell her. "I'm a single child and my parents pretty much abandoned me."

"Oh my god," she says with a gasp. "That's terrible."

"I was a teenager," I continue with a deep breath. "I was in grade eight and my father got a big job offer in Tokyo. He took it and instead of bringing me with them, my parents shoved me into a boarding school, left, and never looked back."

She reaches across the table and puts her hand on mine. "I'm so sorry, Duncan."

"They paid the school, but that's about it. No phone calls, no visits, not even a birthday card. I stayed there over the holidays and over the summer with the other rejected kids. I took it hard. It seemed like every day I'd get into a fight with the rich preppy kids and then be dragged into the principal's office even though they were the ones who jumped me."

She rubs my hand with her thumb, encouraging me with her eyes to go on. I didn't think I'd ever talk about this with anyone. I thought it was locked up in my past for good, but this angel has a way of making me want to open up to her. I want to tell her everything.

"By the time I graduated, all I wanted to do was be on my own. I traveled around, working odd jobs here and there, and then one day my parents' lawyer caught up with me.

Yearning In The Mountains

They died in a train accident in Kyoto. I got a big inheritance and settled down here in the Greene Mountains. I got my house built and kept to myself. I volunteer to plow the mountain roads in the winter since they can never find anyone to do it, and that's been all I needed. I never wanted anything else. Until now..."

Her back straightens as we stare into each other's eyes. We both know a connection like this doesn't come around very often. Once in a lifetime, if you're lucky.

I'm not about to let it go.

"Make room," April grunts as she arrives with our plates.

We're forced to release each other's hands as she dumps the food in front of us. But our bodies are like magnets now—they have to be constantly touching.

Our feet find each other under the table and they stay that way for the rest of the amazing meal.

🍥

"I could spend every night like this," Vivian says with a contented sigh as she looks up at the bright stars shining over our heads. We're sitting in front of a campfire in my backyard after dinner. There's soft music playing and she's cuddled up under a blanket since it's a chilly night. "I mean... Not that I'd... You know what I mean."

Those alert blue eyes flash over to me. I smile at her, trying to put her at ease.

"You're welcome to stay as long as you'd like," I tell her in a soft voice.

She swallows hard as she watches me closely. "For the week, right?"

I shake my head. "I want you to stay, Vivian. Forever.

You're the one for me. I already know it through and through."

"After only a couple of days?" she asks. "How can you know that for sure?"

"I feel it in my aching soul. I feel it in my pounding heart. With every breath I take, I know that you're the one for me. I'm already obsessed with you, princess. If you're not careful, I won't let you leave."

She smiles, but I'm not sure if I'm joking. I need this woman in my life. If she refuses to stay, I might just have to follow her to New York City.

I suck in a breath as she gets up and unravels the blanket from around her body. She's so fucking sexy. The dark shadows mix with the orange glow of the fire, swaying along her body as she comes to me.

My hard cock aches as she sits in my lap, cuddling up to my chest as I wrap my protective arms around her. I love the smell of her—delicious vanilla that always makes my mouth water.

"I'm crazy for you," I whisper as I thread my fingers through her soft hair. "I'd do anything for you."

She shifts her leg and gasps in shock when she feels my rock hard erection.

"See what you do to me?" I say as she makes no effort to move her thigh away from my arousal. I slowly take her hand and put it on my cock. She stops breathing as she feels my hard shaft. "See how fucking hard you make me? I'm going to die without you, girl."

"It's so big," she whispers as that mischievous little hand starts moving up and down my length.

My head drops back and I let out a growl as she strokes me.

Yearning In The Mountains

"I've never seen one," she says in a breathless tone, "in real life before."

"You're a virgin?" I ask, my heart stopped as I wait for her answer.

She turns away and slowly nods. "Yeah. Do you think it's weird that I'm a twenty-four-year-old virgin?"

I cup her jaw and tilt her head up until she's looking into my eyes. "I think it's fate. We're meant to be together, princess. You were waiting for your man. You were waiting for *me*."

That hand keeps moving along my rigid shaft as I kiss her open mouth with a fierce intensity and desire burning through my body. She whimpers against my tongue as I taste her sweet mouth.

"Can I... see it?" she asks when I pull away.

"It's yours, baby. You can do whatever you want to it."

Her eyes light up with excitement as she slides off my lap and drops to her knees.

I'm breathing heavily—watching in awe as she unbuckles my belt. My cock is *throbbing* in my pants. I've never been this turned on.

She opens my belt and then pulls down my zipper. I swallow hard as she reaches into my underwear and pulls out my big hard cock.

"*Wow*," she whispers as she stares at it towering in front of her shocked face.

It looks so big in her hands. I never realized how large it was until now. It looks wildly disproportionate to her body and I'm worried it's going to hurt her too much.

She squeezes the thick base of my shaft and slides her hand up my length, watching with mesmerized lust-filled eyes as a drop of creamy pre-cum beads at the tip.

"Look at the mess you're causing," I say with a growl. "Open that mouth and clean your man up."

She licks her lips as she stares at my dick like she's incapable of looking away.

I groan as she suddenly leans forward and takes me into her mouth. She's a little too eager and takes me in too fast. She shoves me in way too deep and starts choking.

Those sexy blue eyes water as she pulls me out and struggles to catch her breath. I've never seen a sexier sight. Her hand is still gripping my shaft like she's never going to let it go.

My cock is shining with her saliva as she tries a different approach. She places that hot wet tongue on the base of my cock and drags it all the way up.

"*Oh, fuck,*" I groan as I watch her slide it around my head before taking me back into her mouth. She goes easier this time, taking me a little bit at a time until her mouth is completely stuffed with my cock.

"*Yes,*" I growl as she sucks me off, moving her head up and down my length. "Just like that, princess."

I know I'm not going to last long. Her soft warm mouth feels too fucking good.

And the sight of my sexy girl with her virgin lips wrapped around my hard dick is enough to push me over the edge all on its own.

I slide my hands into her hair, grab her head, and move her hot mouth up and down my length faster. I'm being too rough with her, but I can't seem to stop myself. I've lost all control.

"*Fuck,*" I growl as I pull my hands off her head, not wanting to hurt her. But even without me forcing her mouth down, she doesn't stop taking me in deep.

She eagerly sucks my cock until I'm squeezing my

hands into fists as the most intense orgasm of my life comes raging forward.

I cum with a loud savage *roar*.

My load surges into her mouth and she drinks every drop of it down with sharp hungry moans.

Long after the last jolt of my cock, she's still sucking me softly, moaning as she cups my balls in her hand.

"You're perfect," I whisper as I stare at her in awe. "I'm sorry if I was too rough. I wasn't trying to hurt you."

She pulls me out and kisses my shaft. "I know. And don't worry, you could never be too rough."

I watch her with ravenous eyes as she stands up and wipes her wet lips with the back of her hand. I wonder how wet her pussy is right now. The thought of it dripping with need makes me growl with hunger.

"Goodnight, Duncan. I'll see you tomorrow," she says before quickly darting away and disappearing into the house.

My mouth drops open as I watch her go.

I guess I won't be tasting that sweet, honey-filled pussy tonight. But tomorrow... Tomorrow, I won't let her get away this easily.

Tomorrow, I'll make this hot little virgin *mine*.

Chapter Six

Vivian

I catch myself smiling in the mirror after my shower in the morning. I never smile in the morning. I'm always going over my busy calendar, preparing for another stressful day.

I've barely thought about work once since I've been here. Duncan Dove is keeping me all kinds of distracted.

Now that I have work on my mind, I can't help but go through my phone and look at my emails. Over three hundred. Forty-nine are marked urgent.

"Nope," I say as I shut it off and toss it back into the bottom of my suitcase where it's been all week. I don't want to deal with any of that. Not today, not this week, not ever. A growing part of me never wants to open that email account again.

My thoughts quickly return to Duncan as I get myself

ready for the day. I can't believe I gave him a blow job last night. Something unexpected came over me and I just dropped to my knees, wanting to please him so badly.

But I think I enjoyed it even more than he did. My fingertips tingle as I remember the feeling of having that hard pulsing cock in my hand.

This hot mountain man has his hooks in me. I can't stop thinking about him and dreaming about all the tantalizing what-ifs.

What if I stay? What if we belong together? What if I throw caution to the wind and let him have me?

I shiver from the enticing thought.

He's so fun to be around, so fucking sexy, and sometimes I feel like he knows me better than I know myself.

He knows what makes me tick. It's like he can see through all the layers and walls I've built up over the years. He sees the true me. The real me. The me that is lonely. The me that does want more.

The me that wants the kind of life that he can provide—children, a loving family, a safe home in a stunning natural paradise.

A knock on the door makes me jump.

"Yeah?"

"Breakfast is ready," he says through the door. That deep voice has my body purring already. I love hearing his voice traveling through the house. It's like a big warm masculine blanket wrapping around me.

"I'll be right there," I say, quickly fixing my hair.

My heart pounds with anticipation as I head down the hall. Duncan is in the kitchen cutting strawberries. He smiles as I walk in and I realize that there's no other place in the world I'd rather be than here in this kitchen with him.

"I hope you like crepes with *real* maple syrup," he says as he washes his hands.

"What's not to like?" I ask with my stomach grumbling as I pull out a stool and sit at the island.

"Good, then eat up," he says as he joins me. "We're going on a *big* hike today. We're climbing a mountain."

I'd like to climb him instead.

"A mountain?" I say with a gulp. "A big one?"

"The biggest."

"Think a city girl can handle it?" I ask teasingly.

He grins. "After last night, I don't think there's anything too big for you to handle."

My cheeks get all red and hot at the double entendre. "Maybe," I say as I flash him a playful glare. "Or, maybe it wasn't as big as you think."

He laughs, not self-conscious at all. I guess if you have a cock as big as he does, you don't get self-conscious with jokes about its size. It's as big as they come.

"I checked out your fashion line," he says as he turns back to the stove. He takes a crepe off the pan, lays it out on a plate, places some cut strawberries along the center, then wraps it up and places it in front of me. "Don't forget the syrup. Your clothes are beautiful."

"You looked up my brand?" I ask, getting nervous as I drown the crepe in maple syrup. "When?"

"Last night. I googled it. When are you going to make men's clothes? I'd buy up the store."

"I don't think my factory has enough material to cover your giant frame."

He laughs. "Seriously though, Vivian. I'm impressed. You're so talented and the fact that you built up a successful brand and a fashion empire by twenty-four years old… You're amazing."

I look at him to see if he's teasing me, but he's not. He's dead serious.

"It would be amazing if the clothes were environmentally sustainable," I say with a sigh. "I'm not loving that I'm contributing to fast fashion."

"Stop. You're incredible. And if you want to start over in the future, there's nothing stopping you from giving it another go and implementing the lessons you've learned along the way."

That would be amazing. Just selling it all and walking away clean and worry-free. I could spend some time out here, maybe with Duncan if he's interested, and eventually start over with a sustainable luxury brand for outdoorsy people. I keep looking at Duncan's big muscular frame and picturing all sorts of nice clothes on him.

"Maybe," I whisper as I stab a piece of strawberry and crepe with my fork. I bring it to my mouth and *oh my god!* "This is the best thing I've ever had in my mouth!"

He grins at me like it's too easy. "I hope it's not the *best* thing..."

And I finish the crepe with my cheeks blushing darker than ever.

I'm sweating buckets by the time we're two-thirds of the way up the trail. And out of breath. And desperate for a break.

Duncan is barely bothered at all by the heat and the insane incline of the mountain. His shirt has a little bit of sweat on his chest, but it just makes him look even sexier. Meanwhile, I have streams dripping down my face and my tank top has big gross wet circles under my armpits. I must look like a wreck.

"How often do you do this?" I ask in a breathless tone. I also have a sharp jutting pain in my ribs and it hurts to speak.

"Hiking?" he asks, speaking as easily as he did at breakfast. "Pretty much every day. I love getting out here in the mountains. It's food for the soul."

"Totally," I say, holding in a wheeze.

It is beautiful. The views are incredible and I love being under all of these tall trees. I would like to be as fit and able as Duncan though. One day, I'll be able to keep up with him and barely break a sweat. One day...

"Is that a river?" I ask when I hear flowing water in the distance.

"Yeah, come check it out."

We step off the trail and hike through the forest until we emerge next to some giant rocks next to the river, some taller than me. Beyond the massive rocks is a gorgeous river of crystal-clear water. It looks so tempting and refreshing as it runs over smooth river rocks before gathering into little natural pools all over the place. My hot sweltering body *craves* it.

Duncan seems to notice my yearning for it and grins. "Want to cool off?"

"You mean go swimming?"

"Yeah."

He pulls off his shirt and my eyes practically bulge out of my head when I see his muscular torso for the first time. It's unreal.

My dry mouth begins to water as I'm treated to the sexy view of his massive chest and shredded abs. I don't know where to look. My eyes zero in on his neck tattoo that finishes on the top of his chest and continues along his big round shoulders and down his muscular arms.

He's so fucking hot. This man should be a model. He should be a movie star. He should have millions of women obsessed with him, but I know he wouldn't be happy with any of that. He's a natural-born recluse who loves being in the mountains and I'm glad for that. I kind of like having him all to myself. He's my own hidden secret.

"Are you going in?" I ask as he takes off his shoes. I like how his arms flex and tighten when he reaches down and pulls them off. Lucky for me, he's wearing two shoes, so I get to see it again.

"Yeah, and so are you."

"I don't have a bathing suit."

"I think we're past bathing suits," he says, standing back up as he looks at me. "We both saw everything there is to see."

"Yeah, but..."

He waits for me to finish. I have nothing. No good argument. No reason why I shouldn't get naked in front of this beautiful man that I'm falling for. So, I just think 'To hell with it' and kick off my shoes and pull off my tank top.

He swallows hard as he watches me unbutton my shorts and wiggle them down my hips. I step out of them and pull my socks off at the same time.

When I stand back up, I'm wearing nothing but my bra and underwear. Duncan's eyeing me with a look so hungry it gives me tingles.

"Let me get the rest," he says in a thick gravelly voice.

I shiver as he walks up to me and reaches around my back. He smells like the mountains—fresh soil and pine with some masculine testosterone thrown in. I breathe in his erotic scent as he unclasps my bra with his powerful hand.

The birds are singing overhead like it's any regular old morning, completely oblivious to the erotic event happening down here.

Our eyes are on each other as he slowly pulls my bra off. I've never willingly shown a man this part of me before, but I want him to see it. For the first time in my life, I want to be naked with a man. I want him to see everything.

He never breaks eye contact as he slides my bra down my arms and tosses it onto one of the giant rocks beside us. My breasts tumble free. My nipples harden in the fresh mountain air now that they're in the open.

Duncan inhales and then holds his breath as he slowly drags his eyes down. He sees my naked breasts for the second time this week, but you'd swear it was the first by the way his eyes aren't blinking and how he's seemingly forgotten how to breathe.

"You're beautiful," he says as he reaches up and cups them in his strong rough hands. I drop my head back and moan as he leans down and takes a hard tingling nipple into his mouth.

His beard is all scratchy on my skin, which just heightens the sensation of his warm soft mouth on me.

"Oh, Duncan," I moan as I run my fingers through his hair, holding his mouth against me. He switches his ravenous lips to my other breast and sucks my nipple until my pussy is soaked and begging for some attention.

I'm swaying to the rhythm of his tongue, pulling him against me as I imagine that beautiful dick all hard and ready for me. I reach down and feel for it. It doesn't take long to find that big towering rod jutting out against the inside of his shorts.

He groans as I stroke his length with my flat palm, up and down, up and down.

Those big strong hands slide to the back of my body and then come down onto my ass with a firm grip. I whimper as I feel his strength squeezing and pulling my ass cheeks apart. I'm so fucking wet. My pussy is *throbbing* for this man.

I want him so badly I can't think straight. I want him in me. I want him to possess and own me. I want him to take it all and never give it back.

My heart pounds as I unbuckle his belt. His hot tongue traces one nipple and then the other. It feels so good.

His shorts fall down and I immediately reach into his boxer briefs and wrap my hand around his thick hot shaft. I give it a squeeze and he groans.

The heavy pulse between my legs is smoldering hot. I'm *so* wet. I'm so ready to surrender to his mercy. I'm overcome with lust that I forget I'm all sweaty and gross.

Then it clicks.

"I gotta jump in the water first," I tell him through heavy breaths. I try to pull away, but his strong hands keep me in place.

"No, you don't."

"I'm gross," I say, wanting to leave, but melting against that hot tongue as it circles my breast again.

"You're anything but gross." With the way he's looking at me right now, I just might believe him. He drags his tongue up my neck with a hungry groan. "You're so fucking tasty. I love your natural scent. Your natural taste. Don't run away from me. *Please.* I need you so badly."

Those hands grip my panties and he tears them off with a hard tug. I gasp as they fall away in tatters.

"I can't wait another second, princess," he growls with a carnal look in his dark brown eyes. "I *need* you. I need to be in you."

"I need you too," I whisper as I pull down his boxer briefs.

He pushes me up against the closest giant rock and hovers over me, gripping his hard cock as I look up at him breathlessly.

This is it. He's going to take my virginity.

He can fucking have it. I don't want it anymore. I just want him.

Duncan grabs the back of my knee and pulls my leg up as I lean back on the incline of the large boulder, looking at him as my heart pounds in anticipation.

The beautiful head of his cock which felt so big and wide in my mouth feels even bigger as he presses it to my virgin opening.

I gasp as he adds some pressure, sliding the thick tip inside my tight throbbing pussy.

"*Yes*," I whisper as I cling to his sweaty muscular body. "I want *more*."

He slowly pushes those strong hips forward, sliding his cock deeper into me until my pussy is engulfing all of his thick head.

A shiver rushes through me to the tips of my curled toes as he grabs the back of my neck. Our foreheads touch and we stare into each other's eyes—mouths open, breathing quick shallow breaths—as he pushes in one hard thick inch at a time.

A warm sweet pain fills my pussy. He's so big, but I don't want him to stop. I would die if he stopped now.

His giant cock arrives at my cheery and he grits his teeth before thrusting through it. I scream out. My nails dig into his arms. His cock slides all the way in to the hilt and I'm unable to breathe as he fills me up for the first time.

"You're mine now," he growls in my ear as he holds his giant dick inside me.

I'm clinging on to him, desperately trying to get used to his tremendous size.

"I think I've always been yours," I whisper back.

He kisses me on the mouth and then starts moving his hips, thrusting in and out of me and bringing me to heights higher than I ever thought possible...

Chapter Seven

Duncan

I'm trying to go easy on this beautiful little virgin pussy, but it's damn near impossible. The tight squeeze is making my jaw clench as I thrust my hips back and forth, fucking my beauty too hard for her first time.

Her mouth opens and she lets out a sexy little whimper as I drive in deep, burying my hard cock in her tight little heat.

She's so fucking sexy. I'm overwhelmed with all of the exquisite places to look from her bouncing naked tits to her moaning face to her soft flawless skin running along every inch of her. But above all, my eyes keep darting to the hottest thing I've ever seen—my cream-covered cock sliding back and forth between her parted pink pussy lips.

"You like that, princess?" I growl as I drive in deep. "I

know you do. You love taking every inch of my thick cock, don't you?"

She rolls the back of her head on the rock as her eyes fall closed. "I fucking love it. You feel so good inside me, Duncan. Don't stop, *please*."

I slide my hand up her ribs and grab her bouncing tit with a hard firm grip. She whimpers as her perky nipple digs into my palm.

"This pussy is mine now," I say with my lips hovering over her open mouth. "You're never taking it away from me."

"I won't..."

"You're staying here, princess. You're staying with me where I can take you every, single, day."

Her nails dig into my tattooed flesh as I hit her hard with four punishing thrusts.

A fresh wave of hot cream leaks onto my balls.

It drives me crazy. It makes me primal. I feel like a caveman who's lost all shred of civility as I fuck her harder. Carnal instincts take over.

I want to *breed* this woman.

I need to fill her fresh ripe womb with my seed. My balls are aching as I picture her walking around, belly swollen, my child growing inside her.

There's nothing between us—nothing stopping me from doing just that. No condom. No birth control. Nothing.

Once the thought is in my head, it takes over. It consumes me.

I need to *breed* this beauty.

"That's my girl," I whisper as I drive my hard cock into her little cunt. "There's one more thing I need from you."

"*Anything*," she gasps.

"I'm going to count down from ten and when I get to

one—and not before one—I want you to make this sweet little pussy cum all over my dick."

She whimpers, her face tightening like there's no way she can wait that long. My girl is already teetering on the edge. It's going to be torture for her to hold it in, but then it will be that much sweeter when she finally does let go.

"Can you do that for me?"

"I'll try," she whimpers.

I grab her jaw and tilt her head up with enough force that her startled blue eyes snap up to mine. "Not until one."

She nods her head.

"That's my girl. Ten."

I release her jaw and drag my tongue up her neck, tasting her sweet salty essence. "Nine."

"Oh shit, Duncan. Oh shit..."

I slide in and out of her heat with long fast strokes. My balls are aching they're so full. I don't know if I can last this long either.

"Eight."

I grab under her knees and lift her up. She gasps as I spread her legs apart, letting gravity pull her down onto my dick as I hold her against the rock.

"That's it, baby. Seven. You're doing amazing."

Somehow she's even tighter like this. I grit my teeth and groan as I slide deep into her.

"Six."

Sharp quick breaths rip in and out of her chest as she struggles to hold her orgasm back. It looks like she's right on the edge.

"You want to cum, don't you?"

"So badly," she whimpers. "Hurry."

I grin as I make her wait for it.

"Don't let go, princess. I need you to wait."

She groans in frustration as I slide in and out at a quick steady pace.

"Five."

More wet juice leaks out. This girl is killing me.

"Four."

Her tits jerk violently back and forth as I pick up the pace.

"I want to cum so bad," I say as I feast my eyes on her. "I'm so fucking close. Three."

"I can't wait any longer," she moans, looking like it's unbearable for her. "Please let me cum. *Please.*"

"Not yet, not yet, not yet. Two. We're so close, baby. Just a little longer."

I know as soon as I say the number, she's going to erupt all over my dick. I know I'll cum too and then our first time will be over.

She'll be bred and her virginity will be mine, but I want to make it last just a little bit longer.

I want to savor the moment as long as I can.

She screams out in agony and frustration as I make her wait. Her body is all tight and rigid like it's taking everything she has to hold the intense powerhouse of an orgasm back.

My chest is so tight. My balls are ready to burst.

"That's my girl. So close. So fucking close."

"*Duncan...*" she whines. "*Please...*"

I grin as I watch how desperate I've made her. I've turned this sweet little virgin into a sex-crazed maniac and there's no going back.

It's time to let her have it. It's time to breed my sexy little virgin.

I hover my mouth over hers, close enough that our lips are grazing each other with each powerful thrust of my hips.

"One."

She clings to me and screams out as her whole body erupts. The tight walls of her pussy constrict around my thick shaft as she cums all over me for the first time.

I want to wait it out. I want to watch her face as she gives in to the pleasure. But it feels so damn good that I can't hold it back.

My orgasm comes hard and fast, tearing through me like a wild bull as I cling to her just as desperately as she's clinging to me.

I hold my big dick inside her pussy and release…

Hot cum surges out of my cock and fills her ripe virgin womb.

Now, she's really mine.

Now, I'll never let her go.

She takes every drop of my seed, moaning as she watches me with those lust-filled blue eyes.

I dig in as my cock takes one last jolt.

Exhaustion hits after the intensity of our orgasms fades through our bodies. I slowly lower her trembling legs until her feet are back on the forest floor.

The birds continue singing over our heads as if the entire world didn't just change. The river keeps gurgling as it flows like the universe hasn't just been altered.

Everything has changed.

My seed is growing in my girl's womb. Her virginity is mine.

Nothing will ever be the same again.

She looks up at me through half-closed eyes as I linger inside her. Finally, I pull out and we both wince.

"You're incredible," I whisper as I hold her close, not ready to let her go just yet.

"I guess that makes two of us," she says, smiling softly as I hold her in my arms. "Should we go swimming now?"

I lower my lips onto her collarbone and breathe in her intoxicating scent. "In a minute," I whisper. "I'm not ready to let you go just yet."

"Take all the time you need," she whispers back. "I'm good right here."

I hope that's not a lie.

Because what I need is her in my arms forever.

Chapter Eight

Duncan

Vivian doesn't know it, but I've been asking around town, trying to find the guy who scammed her with the fake rental. If she actually leaves at the end of the week, which I'm hoping she won't, she'll be leaving with her money.

I know this crook is from the Greene Mountains. He used actual pictures of my house for the listing, so that means he's been on my secluded road taking photos.

I've been texting some guys I know from around town about this Kyle Kline. I figured it was an alias, but apparently, the guy is even stupider than I thought. He didn't even make up a fake name, the moron. My buddy Julian from the Search and Rescue team overheard him bragging about scamming 'some dumb bitch' in the bar.

I'm headed there right now to teach him some manners.

Vivian is still sleeping at home. I left her a note next to the pot of coffee saying that I'll be back soon.

I pull up to the address I was given and grit my teeth when I see his rundown trailer with all of the garbage scattered around his wild mess of a property.

"Wakey wakey, motherfucker," I whisper as I step out of my truck and slam the door closed.

I march up to the door with my body tense and my heart racing. I pound on the door repeatedly until he yanks it open a minute later.

He's a scrawny punk with the shittiest tattoos I've ever seen and some of the mangiest messy hair around. He yawns so loud I can see all of his missing teeth and then he scowls at me. "What the fuck do you want?"

I grab a fistful of his hair and yank him down the steps. He trips on the stairs and falls to the ground by my feet.

"What the fuck, man?!" he screams as I grip his hair tighter.

"Do you know me?"

"No!" he screeches. "I've never seen you in my life, man! Let me go! Fuck!"

I kick him in the ribs. "Then why the fuck did you take pictures of my house and put them online?"

"I didn't!"

"I know it was you, Kyle. You stole money from a very important person to me."

"I steal money from a lot of people, man," he whines as he tries to get away from my grip. He can't. "Don't take it so personally."

I kick him in the ribs again. "You don't steal from *her*."

"Alright, fuck man. Just let me go."

"I want her money back. Thirteen hundred dollars."

"Thirteen hundred dollars?! I don't have that kind of coin."

I yank him up to his feet, slam his back against the trailer, and punch him as hard as I can in the stomach. He folds in half with a gurgling sound and then falls to his knees, clutching his stomach as he tries to catch his breath.

"We're going to do this until I get her money."

"Fuck, man," he says with a wheeze. "Is it that dumb bitch who booked the cottage?"

"The *what?*" I ask as I show him my fist. He flinches.

"The company blocked my account!" he says, flinching away from me. "I never got the money!"

"Bullshit. She never got a refund, but she's going to get one now. Where is it?"

He doesn't want to tell me, but I can tell he's lying. I cock my fist back and he breaks. "Okay, okay! It's under my sink. Shit, man. That's *my* money. She gave it to me. I *earned* it."

I don't have time to explain to this guy how stealing money is not the same as earning it. I only have a few more hours with my girl and I don't want to waste any more of them with this punk.

"Stay right fucking here," I growl at him before charging into his trailer and heading right to the sink. The place is a disaster and I have to hold my breath so I don't pass out from the smell. There's an old coffee can full of bills under the sink.

I count out thirteen hundred dollars, shove it into my pocket, and then charge back out.

"Next time you commit a felony, don't use your real name, you dumb fuck."

"The site made me verify my license to sign up," he says like that makes it any better.

I shake my head as I walk to my truck. "If I see you on my mountain again," I warn him. "I'll fucking throw you off it."

He's still on his knees as I start my truck and race home to my girl.

Chapter Nine

Vivian

"This has been the best week of my life," I say to Duncan as we sit in the hot tub after dinner. It's another quiet gorgeous night with the stars shining like diamonds over our heads. My muscles are sore all over from the week of hiking, horseback riding, mountain biking, kayaking, and of course from riding this big strong hulking mountain man every chance I've gotten.

"I'll say it to you again, Vivian," Duncan says as he runs a wet hand through his hair, slicking it back just how I like it. "Stay with me. Don't go home."

"But..."

I can see the urgency in his eyes. The desperation. This man is in love with me.

Just like I'm in love with him.

"You can't go," he says as he glides through the water and grips my body with his big hands. There's a determined look in his eyes as he hovers his face a few inches from mine. "You belong here with me. Sell your company. Marry me. Start a family with me. You have to see that this is the only answer. This is fate."

"I..."

I want to believe him. I want to say yes, but it's only been a few days. I... I'm so confused and his gorgeous brown eyes aren't helping the matter.

I know he'll take care of me. I know he'll do whatever he can to keep me safe. He even got my money back from the asshole who scammed me, which I didn't think was possible. He'll be my guardian and protector. He'll die before he lets me get hurt.

"I was wrong when I called you a city girl," he says as he clings to me under the water. "You're a mountain girl, through and through. I can see it so clearly now. I saw your face light up every time you were in the forest, in every river, on every lake. You belong in the mountains, Vivian. You belong with me."

I can't imagine leaving this place. Every time I think about getting on that train and heading to the airport, I feel nauseous.

How can I go back to New York City knowing this amazing man is on the other side of the country? How can I go back to my lonely apartment when I can be in this glorious hot tub with this perfect man? And how can I go back to my soul-sucking job after knowing I had the chance to give it all up and come live in this beautiful mountain town with the man of my dreams?

He inches forward slowly, his lips floating over mine. "Stay with me, baby. Don't make me tie you to my bed for the rest of eternity. Be with me. Be my girl. Let me be your man."

Yearning In The Mountains

I moan when his bottom lip grazes mine. I can taste his hot breath and it's making me all lightheaded and woozy.

I tilt my chin up, trying to get a kiss, but he tilts his head away, torturing me.

"What do you say?" he whispers.

"I... I... I'll stay."

His grip tightens on me. "Really? You mean it?"

How can I say no? How can I leave? I can't. I do belong here with him. There's no place I'd rather be.

"I mean it," I say, feeling a swell of relief filling me up. Now that I've made it, I know it's the right choice. "I want to be yours."

He lunges forward and kisses me like he's never kissed me before. I moan against his tongue as he claims my mouth with an eager intensity that leaves my head spinning.

"I'll make sure that you're grateful for this decision every day of your life."

Those big demanding hands are suddenly turning me around. He pulls down the bottoms of my bikini as I'm pressed up against the edge of the hot tub, bent over with my heart pounding.

"You won't regret a thing."

I already don't. I'm already happier than I've ever been.

His massive palms squeeze my bare ass cheeks as he positions himself behind me. My pussy is completely exposed in front of my mountain man's ravenous eyes. I blush, knowing he can see every last bit. My pussy begins to *throb* as he lets out a low hungry growl at the sight.

There's no urge to hide or take it away. Duncan has opened up a new side of me. A side that loves it when he looks at me down there. This fierce new side wants him to *take* my aching pussy. It can't get enough of him and his towering cock.

With another hungry growl, my man lunges on me with a hunger that sends shivers racing up my arched spine.

His mouth connects with my tingling pussy and it's like warm lightning shooting through my veins. I drop my head with a moan as I feel his powerful tongue thrust inside me. His lips and tongue... they're *everywhere*. Unrelenting and unstoppable as he devours me like he's desperate to get me off.

"*Oh shit,*" I moan as the pleasure heightens. I glance at him over my shoulder and our eyes meet. His whole body is tense and rigid like he's feeling the same intense bliss as I am.

Never in a million years did I think I'd end up with a big rugged man like Duncan. I always thought I'd end up with a nerdy intellectual type or some shy quiet accountant.

I never knew that what I secretly yearned for was the strong confident alpha type. Someone whose testosterone is only outmatched by his strength. Someone who can live on a mountain and can squat the trunk of an old oak tree.

Duncan is better than anyone I could have ever dreamed up on my own.

Now that I know he's the one for me, I'm glad that I never settled for anyone else.

"You taste so *good*," he moans as he tongues my aching clit.

My toes are curled in the water, my eyes squeezed shut. I'm so close to cumming all over his bearded mouth.

I'm gripping the edge of the hot tub as the bubbles rise up all around us. His strong hands pull my ass cheeks apart and he dives in deeper, tonguing my pussy like he's trying to pull the strongest orgasm I've ever had out of me.

It works.

The orgasm comes out of nowhere and hits me so hard I

scream out his name. My senses drown in the pleasure. My back arches as I scream again, tears streaming down my cheeks as the heat—the beautiful heat—emanates from my pussy and then sears through my body shooting all the way down to my toes.

I'm shaking when it's all over. Trembling uncontrollably as I cling to the smooth edge of the hot tub.

I've barely caught my breath before Duncan rises from the water with his big hard dick in his hand.

"*Oh fuck*," I whisper as he grabs my hip and guides his thick head to my tingling pussy lips. I'm so wet that he slides in easily even though he's way too big for me.

I moan at the beautiful sensation of my pussy being so full. His perfect cock fills every inch of it.

I'm not going to last long... I already feel another powerful orgasm about to snap inside of my body. He pulls them out of me so easily. It's like he knows just what to do to make me explode.

His hard grip on my hips, his deep sexy grunts, the force of being rocked back and forth as he thrusts in and out like he can't get enough... It's all too much.

The water splashes violently around us as Duncan thrusts in *harder, deeper*, making me his.

His hard cock hits the right spot inside of me and I scream out as the damn holding back my orgasm breaks and I'm suddenly flooded with waves of heated bliss and pleasure.

My man lodges his firm cock inside my pulsating pussy and releases his hot load *deep* inside me.

I drop my head down and moan when I feel him cumming in my body. I love this feeling... I can't get enough of it.

He holds himself inside me until the last drop has

exited his body and entered mine. Only then do his hands loosen on my hips. He takes a heavy breath and lets out a low groan.

"I'm sorry if I was too rough," he whispers as he pulls out and sinks into the water.

I turn around and slide my limp body down until the hot water is up to my neck.

He's always apologizing for being too rough, but I love it. I wouldn't change a thing. I love feeling his strength on me. It makes me feel irresistible, like he can't hold himself back no matter how hard he tries.

I glide through the water and settle on his lap, moaning as he wraps those big delicious tattooed arms around me.

"I like it like that," I whisper as he holds me like he's never going to let me go. "It feels good."

He kisses my forehead and moans as he holds me against his beating heart.

This right here... This makes my decision easier.

There will be no second thoughts, doubts, or changing of my mind.

This is all I need.

This is all I want.

Right here in the mountains with Duncan...

This is everything.

Epilogue

Vivian

Two years later...

"What's taking you so long?" I ask with a grin as I look down the trail at Duncan who's trailing behind.

I still remember the first time he took me up here. It was a day of a lot of firsts. I was sweating like crazy and could barely keep up with him. But look at me now—I'm not even breaking a sweat!

"I let you take the lead because the view is so much better with you up ahead," he says with a grin.

"Yeah, right," I say, rolling my eyes playfully as I let him catch up.

Our little bambino is strapped to his back, smiling at me over Duncan's big shoulder.

"What do you think, Max?" I ask him as they approach. "Do you think Daddy's letting Mommy win or is he getting too old?"

He squeals in delight and smacks Duncan's big shoulder.

"He agrees with me," I say with a shrug. "You heard it yourself."

Duncan walks right up to me with a stern look. I hold my ground, glaring up at him with my hands on my hips as he towers over me.

"You're lucky I have a one-year-old strapped to my back or I'd make you pay for those words."

My whole body shivers. I love it when Duncan makes me pay for my words. It always involves me bent over something and screaming in bliss while he takes me from behind.

"You can make me pay when we get home," I say with a flirty look. "Maybe when Mr. Maxy here is down for his nap."

Duncan lets out a low growl as he watches me with a hungry look. He reaches for me, but I slip out of his grasp. "*After* Maxy is down for his nap."

I continue up the mountain trail, putting a little more sway in my hips with every step now that I know my hot mountain man husband has his eyes on my ass.

We got married about three days after I decided to stay in the Greene Mountains. It was the best decision of my life.

I sold my fashion company for five million dollars, left New York City, and never looked back. My parents freaked out, but I've been enjoying the space from them. Now, I only have to deal with my mom's craziness once or twice a year when they come visit. It's been nice.

It took no time at all to settle into my new life in this

amazing town with this incredible man. I was pregnant in about two seconds flat and having Max has been a dream come true. He's the best baby in the world. I adore my little family.

But as busy as they keep me, the itch to create is starting to return.

I've been thinking about starting a new fashion brand, but this time, doing it right. Sustainable clothes for environmentally responsible consumers.

They'll be functional, durable, and most importantly, beautiful.

I mentioned it to Duncan the other day and he was fully on board. He wants me to achieve *all* of my dreams. He doesn't want me to have any regrets in life. One of the reasons why I love him so much.

I just have to figure out a way to convince him to be the male model for my brand...

"Mommy!" Max shouts from behind. I smile as I turn around. "Race!"

"You want to race me?"

He nods his big smiling head up and down.

"I don't know... I don't think Daddy is fast enough to catch Mommy."

Max grins even wider. Duncan does too.

My possessive mountain man gets that look in his eye and I turn around with a squeal. I sprint as fast as I can up the trail, but my man still catches me.

He scoops me up in his big arms, tosses me over his shoulder, and continues up the mountain carrying both of us like we weigh nothing at all.

"We all won!" Max says when we arrive at the top of the mountain.

"We sure did," I say as my sexy mountain man lowers

me to my feet, keeping his big protective arms wrapped around me. I look into his beautiful brown eyes, knowing I'm the luckiest woman in the world. "We sure did."

Epilogue

Duncan

Twenty-five years later...

Two and a half decades with this perfect woman and I still yearn for her every second we're apart.

We've made a beautiful life together in the mountains and every day is like a new adventure. It's been a hell of a ride.

"What are you smiling at?" Vivian asks with a grin as she watches me from the other side of the hot tub. Four children later and she's as beautiful as ever. I still catch myself staring at her in awe whenever she walks into the room.

Her beautiful brown hair is tied up in a messy bun on her head as she playfully narrows her blue eyes on me.

"Wouldn't you like to know?" I say with a grin.

"We've been together so long that I already know everything about you, Mr. Dove."

I chuckle. "Is that what you think?"

She tilts her head and grins at me. "That's what I know."

"Alright," I say with a shrug as I look out at our spectacular mountain view. After Vivian's company which makes sustainable clothing blew up in popularity, we could have bought any place in the state, but we stayed here. We both love this house too much to leave.

"Are you holding out on me, Mr. Mountain Man?" she asks as she analyzes me with those sharp blue eyes. "Are you keeping secrets?"

I chuckle when I think back to one secret I've held for a *long* time. "Maybe."

"Tell me."

"What am I going to get out of it?"

She splashes my chest. "*Tell* me."

I run my thumb and index finger over my lips like I'm zippering them up.

She huffs out a breath. "Fine. What do you want?"

I grin as I look at my gorgeous wife. She's fifty-one years old and I wouldn't change a thing about her.

"I'll tell you," I say as those sparkling blue eyes bore into me. "But then I want you to lose the bikini—"

"Of course."

"—Excuse me, I'm not finished."

She crosses her arms and tries to glare at me but I can see that smile peeking through.

"I want you to lose that bikini, come straddle your husband's huge body, slide that sweet little pussy down on my dick, and ride me like you've never ridden me before."

Her breathing hitches and she licks her lips.

"Alright," she says as she raises her chin. "Deal. Now what secret are you keeping from me?"

"The day we met. Do you remember it?"

"How could I forget *that*? I gave you a full frontal flash."

I grin as the image replays in my mind. It's burned into my brain. I still remember every stunning detail of that moment.

"After, I took you to the Greene Mountain Lodge."

"Yeah..."

"And it was fully booked."

"Okay?"

"The secret is..." I drag it out, torturing her. "I called ahead and booked every last room so you'd have to stay with me."

Her mouth drops open and she stares at me in shock.

I can't help but laugh.

She shakes her head as she smiles at me, cheeks flushing like the day we met.

"Why am I not surprised?" she finally says. "You, Mr. Dove, are a scoundrel."

"No. I just always get what I want and what I wanted was you."

She smiles as she gazes into my eyes. I always feel like the luckiest man in the world when she looks at me like that.

"We had a deal. The bikini. Lose it."

She sighs with a playful roll of her eyes and then starts to strip.

My cock gets hard as stone as that bikini flies over the edge of the hot tub and my gorgeous naked wife slides over and straddles my lap.

She grabs my thick shaft and moans as she slides down on it.

"You are a scoundrel," she says as she begins to ride my

length, the hot water splashing all around us. "But thank you for booking those rooms."

"I would have booked the whole damn lodge for you."

I would do anything for her.

My wife.

My soul mate.

My city girl turned mountain woman.

My dream come true.

The End!

More Mountain Men!

Lost In The Mountains

Desire In The Mountains

Passion In The Mountains

Found In The Mountains

Grumpy In The Mountains

Yearning In The Mountains

Mountain Man Fixated

Mountain Man Rescued

Mountain Man Taken

My Mountain Man Muse

Mountain Man Box Set

All in Kindle Unlimited!

Come and join my private Facebook Group!

Become an OTT Lover!

www.facebook.com/groups/OTTLovers

Become Obsessed with OTT

Sign up to my mailing list for all the latest OTT news and get a free book that you can't find anywhere else!

OBSESSED
By Olivia T. Turner
A Mailing List Exclusive!

When I look out my office window and see her in the next building, I know I have to have her.

I buy the whole damn company she works for just to be near her.

She's going to be in my office working under me.

Under, over, sideways—we're going to be working together in *every* position.

This young innocent girl is going to find out that I work my employees *hard*.

And that her new rich CEO is already beyond *obsessed* with her.

This dominant and powerful CEO will have you begging for overtime! Is it just me or is there nothing better than a hot muscular alpha in a suit and tie!

All my books are SAFE with zero cheating and a guaranteed sweet HEA. Enjoy!

Go to www.OliviaTTurner.com to get your free ebook of Obsessed

Audiobooks

Check out my complete collection of audiobooks at
www.OliviaTTurner.com!

I'm adding more of your favorite OTT stories all the time!

Come Follow Me...

www.OliviaTTurner.com

- facebook.com/OliviaTTurnerAuthor
- instagram.com/authoroliviatturner
- goodreads.com/OliviaTTurner
- amazon.com/author/oliviatturner
- bookbub.com/authors/olivia-t-turner